Indigo Blume
and the Garden City

Kwame Alexander

Illustrated by JahSun

CAPITAL
BOOKFEST

For Nandi and Samayah
– Kwame Alexander

To those who have planted seeds of faith and
love into the garden of my life
– JahSun

Published by Word of Mouth Books for
the Capital BookFest
Strengthening Families Through Reading
www.KwameAlexander.com
in association with Far-I-Studios, Inc.
www.faristudios.com

For information on school visits and education discounts,
contact Stephanie at ssa@kwamealexander.com

We are grateful for the editorial guidance and direction of Stephanie Stanley,
Joanna Crowell, Marjory Wentworth, and Pressque Editing.

This book was made possible by the generous support of: VINX, Michel Hammes,
Kate Jerome, Donna Maria Smith, Cassandra Hill, Ellie Maas Davis of Pressque Editing,
Earth Fare of Charleston, South Carolina, and the College of Charleston—Carol Ann
Davis, Dr. Trisha Folds-Bennett, Meredith English, Erin Perkins, and Michael Haskins.

The illustrations were created using pencil, colored pencil, ink, and watercolor.
The text of this book was set in Kristen.

Manufactured in the United States of America
10 9 8 7 6 5

Hello Friends!

The book you're holding right now was made with 100% organic thoughts, a lot of eco-friendly affection, and a few carrots. Like good citizens of the planet, we recycled a few cool ideas, but each illustration is all natural. So sit back, enjoy the view— and the music. That's right, we always listen to music when we create. We thought you might like to listen to some of Indigo's favorite songs. Welcome to the world of Indigo Blume.

With love (and a little dirt),

Kwame and JahSun

PS. We'd love to come to your school or library (or even your backyard barbecue, as long as you have some tasty greens).

Indigo Blume skipped to the park,
eating a purple plum.

Halfway there,
she stepped in a wad

of pink peppermint gum.

Wiping her shoe, Indigo thought
"I'll tidy up my street.

I'll pick up trash, recycle cans,
and make the sidewalk neat."

Indigo came upon a sign
outside the pizzeria.
*Go Green Up Your Community
A Prize for Best Idea.*

"A contest for our neighborhood."
She told her friends the news.
"Let's start a rooftop garden club.
There's no way we can lose."

The kids all laughed at her big plan,
and teased poor Indigo.
"You'll never win the contest.
Plants on the roof will never grow."

Feeling blue and kind of sad,
she wandered to the park
to chat with her favorite maple tree,
Professor Woody Bark.

NO SWIMMING

"My neighbors won't participate
in cleaning up the city.
They don't believe a garden space
can make our small town pretty."

"Cheer up, that's quite spectacular,
you're thinking eco-smart."
"Well, thank you Mr. Woody, but
I don't know how to start."

"We do," said DJ Earl the Squirrel and sidekick Roxy Rabbit.

"Just mix some soil with seeds and sun, then rock those nuts and carrots."

Just then, a hummingbird named Zip zooooooooomed onto the scene.

"Don't forget the flowers honey,
nectar's my cuisine."

"To grow the garden of your life,"
Woody Bark professed,
"plant the seeds of faith and love,
let nature do the rest."

The next morning, Indigo Blume
arranged her purple pots.
She wore her green gardener's hat,
for it was blazing hot.

She used organic potting soil
to help the seedlings grow.
Zucchini, berries, pansies, and
tomatoes in a row.

In just one month, the garden grew.
Kids came from near and far
to witness climbing beans so tall,
they almost touched a star.

To celebrate the contest day
Indigo threw a jam.
With music, dance, and lemonade,
plus heaps of greens and yams.

The judges loved Indigo's roof,
and awarded her first prize:

A box and bow so **big and bold,**
she couldn't believe her eyes.

"Indigo won a purple bike!"
The kids all waved and screamed.
"Thanks for brightening Garden City,

and helping us Go Green."

Indigo's Rooftop Garden Glossary

Go Green means to change your lifestyle for the safety and benefit of the environment. People who "go green" make decisions about their daily lives while considering what impact the outcome of those decisions may have on global warming, pollution, and loss of animal habitats among other environmental concerns.

Recycle means to use again, and adapt to a new use or function. Many things we normally throw away can be reused, including paper, glass, metals, plastics, vegetable peelings, and cut grass. Recycling conserves natural resources like trees and energy.

A **Garden** is a plot of land used for growing flowers, vegetables, herbs, or fruit.

A **Rooftop Garden** is any garden on the roof of a building. These gardens may provide food, temperature control, water-related benefits, beautification, and recreational opportunities.

Planting means to place seeds or young plants in the ground.

Fruit is the part of a flowering plant—such as a sweet peach, plum, or pomegranate—that contains seeds.

Vegetables are any edible part of a plant with a savory flavor, such as spinach, carrots, or broccoli.

Maple Trees are very common trees in the United States, and vary in size by species. Some reach only fifteen to twenty feet, while others can grow to seventy feet or more in height.

Meditate means to think or reflect in a relaxed state of mind.

Eco-smart means being healthy, efficient, and environmentally friendly.

Soil is dirt found in the top layer of the earth's surface; plants typically grow in soil.

A **Seed** is a very small organism with a protective coat that will grow into a new plant under the right conditions.

The **Sun** is the star that is the source of light and heat for the plants and humans on planet Earth.

Water is a clear, colorless, odorless, and tasteless liquid essential for most plant and animal life.

Nectar is a sweet liquid produced by the flowers of various plants. Pollinators like hummingbirds and insects eat nectar and bees gather nectar to make honey.

A **Flower** is a plant, such as a tulip or sunflower, cultivated for its blooms or blossoms.

Organic food is healthier for you, because it is grown without pesticides, herbicides, fertilizers, or other additives.

Potting Soil is a mixture used to grow plants, herbs, and vegetables in a contained environment like a rooftop garden.

Seedlings are young plants or trees grown from a seed.

Beans are pod-shaped vegetables, also called legumes, which come in many different shapes and sizes. Examples are lima beans, pinto beans, and climbing beans, which can grow very tall.

Made in the USA
Middletown, DE
10 April 2017